SUNDAY
IN KYOTO

Songs by Gilles Vigneault
Illustrated by Stéphane Jorisch

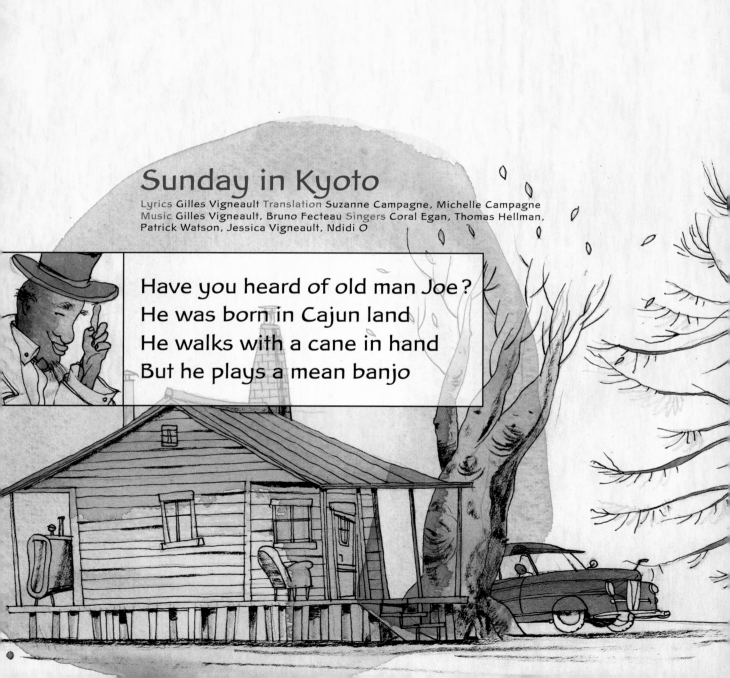

Sunday in Kyoto

Lyrics Gilles Vigneault Translation Suzanne Campagne, Michelle Campagne
Music Gilles Vigneault, Bruno Fecteau Singers Coral Egan, Thomas Hellman,
Patrick Watson, Jessica Vigneault, Ndidi O

Have you heard of old man Joe?
He was born in Cajun land
He walks with a cane in hand
But he plays a mean banjo

Now he lives in Kyoto
For his wife is Japanese
See her fingers dance with ease
Playing notes on the koto

Friends from Spain come by for tea
And they all play the guitar
Yes, the boy is quite bizarre
But he sings *so* beautifully

There's a woman you can see
In a pure white kimono
Obi tied up in a bow
Strumming on her bouzouki

Let me tell you about Yoshi
Fingers dancing on the harp
Has a pond of swimming carp
Just don't say the word "sushi"

Gave a concert, oh so zen
And just as they stood and bowed
Three notes lifted from the crowd
Played upon a shamisen

In attendance you could see
Buddha statues made of bronze
Buddhist monks in their sarongs
Meditating silently

At the final midnight gong
From the forest comes a cry
It's an owl perched up high
Hooting all night long

Then a mouse came out to see
Stood on stage and gave a nod
All the Buddhist monks applaud
Buddhas smiling happily

Joe's Mother

Lyrics Gilles Vigneault Translation Suzanne Campagne, Paul Campagne
Music Gilles Vigneault Singer Jessica Vigneault

Joe's mother, she clucks
While feeding her ducks
They're his, and that's fine
Take yours, I'll take mine.

Yoshi raises geese
He says he's for peace
But I have a hunch
Those geese are for lunch.

Old drunk and his dog
Both snort like a hog
Together, as such
Not worth very much!
(Not much)

If You Bump Your Knee

Lyrics Gilles Vigneault Translation Michelle Campagne
Music Gilles Vigneault, Jessica Vigneault Singer Thomas Hellman

If you bump your knee
Have a cup of tea
Yuuki

If you stub your toe
Hip hop to and fro
Kaito

If your tummy's sore
Lie down on the floor
Igor

If you hurt your back
Walk around the track
Big Jack

Morning Breaks on Skates

Lyrics Gilles Vigneault Translation Suzanne Campagne, Michelle Campagne
Music Gilles Vigneault, Robert Bibeau Singer Ndidi O

Morning breaks
On skates
Noon breeze
On skis
Nights are
Black as tar
Tell me what goes on at night
When the kids are sleeping tight?

The toboggans in the night
Slide away upon the hill
The toboggans in the night
Slide away of their own will
Louis saw them. Yes he did!
Underneath the moon's glow
Louis saw them. Yes he did!
They were his, so he should know!

Morning breaks
On skates
Noon breeze
On skis
Nights are
Black as tar
Tell me what goes on at night
When the kids are sleeping tight?

The toboggans and the skis
Leave no tracks upon the snow
The toboggans and the skis
They are silent as they go
And the skates upon the lake
Twist and twirl but never fall
But the skates upon the lake
Have no feet in them at all!

Morning breaks
On skates
Noon breeze
On skis
Nights are
Black as tar
Tell me what goes on at night
When the kids are sleeping tight?

In the morning we can see
That the sleds are still around
But the skates and all the skis
They are nowhere to be found
You'll find a ski up on the hill
You'll find a skate under a cap
It all depends upon the chill
And if the kids have had their nap

Morning breaks
On skates
Noon breeze
On skis
Nights are
Black as tar

One, Two, Three, ABCD

Lyrics Gilles Vigneault Translation Suzanne Campagne, Paul Campagne, Michelle Campagne Music Gilles Vigneault Singer Thomas Hellman

Ichi, ni, san, shi, go,
Roku, shichi, hachi, kyu, ju

One and two... fire on cue
Three and four... settle a score
Five and six... stones and bricks
Seven, eight, nine... draw the line
Ten, eleven... gone to heaven
Twelve, thirteen... intervene
Fourteen to twenty... stop the bout
Go to your corner, time out!

Un et deux
Trois et quatre
Cinq et six
Sept, huit, neuf
Dix et onze
Douze et treize
Quinze à vingt

A B C D... Old man McGee
E F & G... Says come and see
H I J K... My cow René
L M N O P... All she does is pee!
Q R & S... Oh what a mess!
T U & V... How gross is she!
W X... Oh no, what's next!
Y & Z... She farts instead!

And the old man says, "Pooeee!"

Sleep Tight My Love

Lyrics Gilles Vigneault Translation Suzanne Campagne
Music Gilles Vigneault, Gaston Rochon Singer Coral Egan

Sleep tight, my love, the wind is here
To keep you safe outside till dawn
For horse and ducky, sleep is near
As the nest sways, birdie will yawn
And in the mansion of your ear
A spinning wheel will soon appear
It weaves dreams that you can keep
Of golden sheep
Sleep

Sleep tight, you know the city's there
In open fields where trees belong
The night is young, yet wise and fair
The wolf is far, the wind is strong
A train goes by, the owl stares
A sailing ship appears out there
The port is safe, the water's deep
Just take a leap
Sleep

You can sleep tight now, all is well
It's in this moment that we know
The secrets that time will tell
Only your dreams will make it so
Sleep now, the clock will oversee
The honey harvest of the bee
Bear in a tree, curled in a heap
A forest deep
Sleep

Little Miss Adèle

Lyrics Gilles Vigneault Translation Suzanne Campagne
Music Gilles Vigneault, Jessica Vigneault Singer Patrick Watson

Little Miss Adèle
Sitting in her clothes
With a page in hand
And a pen that glows
Oh...

Writes the letter H
Then an E and L
And another L
Then a little O

Could you be a bird?
Tell me yes or no!
Tell me what's your name?
My name is HELLO!

When the Dance Began

Lyrics Gilles Vigneault Translation Michelle Campagne
Music Gilles Vigneault, Jessica Vigneault Singer Coral Egan

When the dance began
When I heard the music
When the dance began
My foot took the floor
But my shoe shot out
Sailing past the dancers
And my silly shoe
Flew right out the door

When the dance began
When I heard the music
When the dance began
Then I lost my shoe
So I hopped around
Dancing a cotillon
So I hopped around
What more could I do?

Someone found my shoe
Lying by the river
So I tied my shoe
Tightly on my foot
It began anew
To shake and to shiver
And my silly shoe
Still will not stay put

Do You Have Some Coins?

Lyrics Gilles Vigneault Translation Suzanne Campagne
Music Gilles Vigneault, Jessica Vigneault Singer Thomas Hellman

Do you have some coins?
Yes, I have some here
For someone who's dear
To my heart, it's true
So true

Do you know her well?
Sweet as morning dew
Do you know her well?
It's you!

Four Eggs

Lyrics Gilles Vigneault Translation Michelle Campagne
Music Gilles Vigneault, Jessica Vigneault Singer Jessica Vigneault

I just cracked an egg of stone
No yolk, not a joke
There were emeralds inside
Do you know who laid it?
Tell me now, my dear
Do you know who laid it?
It was never clear
It was never clear

I just cracked an egg of wood
No yolk, not a joke
There were little words inside
Do you know who wrote them?
Tell me now, my dear
Do you know who wrote them?
It was never clear
It was never clear

I just cracked an egg of glass
No yolk, not a joke
Found a golden ring inside
Do you know who wore it?
Tell me now, my dear
Do you know who wore it?
It was never clear
It was never clear

I just cracked a chicken egg
With a yolk, and it broke!
And my breakfast was inside
So the rooster said
This way, follow me
So the rooster said
Bon appétit!
Bon appétit!

The Great Big Kite

Lyrics Gilles Vigneault Translation Jessica Vigneault
Music Gilles Vigneault, Robert Bibeau Singer Ndidi O

One day I'll make my great big kite
One side red and one side white
One day I'll make my great big kite
One side red and one side white
A tender side...
One day I'll make my great big kite
Children of the world on its back will climb
And they will hear me
I can see them rise in the morning light

Horses of the wind will pull my kite
Horses red and horses white
Horses of the wind will pull my kite
Horses red and horses white
And piebald horses...
Horses of the wind will pull my kite
We will see the oceans as they fight
For their survival
Swelling up a storm in the moonless night

High above the trees and fields so bright
Birds of red and birds of white
High above the trees, and fields so bright
Birds of red and birds of white
A lyrebird...
High above the trees and fields so bright
Looking for the angry Evil Knight
We will destroy him
With a silent bomb and a silver knife

Fight with fire, blood and spite
Sun so red and sun so white
Fight with fire, blood and spite
Sun so red and sun so white
A sombre sun...
Fight with fire, blood and spite
Clouds are rising up in the falling night
And we'll fly higher
Higher than the heights of the city sights

When we return with hearts of light
One side red and one side white
When we return with hearts of light
One side red and one side white
A human side...
When we return with hearts of light
Then you will say that I had no right
To take your children
On such a dark and dangerous flight

I'll climb back on my great big kite
One red morning, one white night
I'll climb back on my great big kite
One red morning, one white night
A paling sunrise...
I'll climb back on my great big kite
Leaving all your children to lead the fight
For truth and freedom
Tossing up the dice in the hands of time

Yoshi and His Boat

Lyrics Gilles Vigneault Translation Michelle Campagne
Music Gilles Vigneault, Jessica Vigneault Singer Patrick Watson

Yoshi loves to float
Float upon the sea
In a paper boat
Of origami
You see

Does a moonlight dance
What a pretty sight
Wants to sail to France
He will go tonight
Goodnight
Bonsoir

Settler's Lullaby

Lyrics Gilles Vigneault Translation Michelle Campagne
Music Gilles Vigneault, Robert Bibeau Singer Jessica Vigneault

Snow has fallen on the woods
And upon the stream
Buried underneath the weight
Quail and pheasants dream
Sleep, sleep now, baby, sleep now
There's a Jesus golden boy
Born among the Iroquois
Isn't it a wonder?

Wolves and coyotes spread the news
Howling all day long
Foxes turning fiddle wheels
Play a haunting song
Slowly slumber, little dreamer
Caribou have come to see
Watch them bow on bended knee
What a thing of beauty

You will be the trapper King
So the legends say
When they see your fearless face
Wolves will run away
Deeper, deeper, little sleeper
Dive into your gentle dream
See the starlight cast its gleam
You will be a Saviour

The Poem of a Child

Lyrics Gilles Vigneault Translation Suzanne Campagne, Michelle Campagne
Music Gilles Vigneault, Jessica Vigneault Singer Thomas Hellman

Oh... the poem of a child
Is a flea market running wild
We see elephants with kids
Putting their trunks up for bid

And a regimental drum
With pretty Russian dolls
A captain dressing from
Paper ships so white and tall

And a fisherman in rags
Finds captive on his line
Lovely horses made of wood
Tiny slivers oh so fine!

"Shall I give these to the king?"
But the jester with a sigh
Says: "You can't speak to a king!
It's the law, don't ask me why!"

Now the oboe gives the A
Just as one would give the time
And the mouse is with the cat
Shopping for a winter hat

We are sometimes at a loss
For a word that laughs, that cries
When a wolf we come across
Falls asleep before our eyes

But a child when he writes
Won't know he's a poet yet
He's the first to be surprised
By the smiling words he's met

So when a poet writes
Is he still a child within?
When his words race out of sight
Just like horses in the wind

He'll chase words of love and hope
Amidst all the market cries
When they sell bubbles made of soap
Filled with pretty butterflies

With his graceful magic hands
Filled with loaded dice and stuff
The magician scams his fans
'Cause he can and that's enough

In a kiosk on its own
There's a child selling poems
Underneath the watchful eye
Of an old man standing by

And he'll sell love letters too
For their words will make us sigh
They'll say "Stay with me" and "I d
"Bon voyage" and then "Goodbye

In his finest writing yet
He'll make words we won't forget

Record Producer Paul Campagne Artistic Director Roland Stringer
Illustrations Stéphane Jorisch Designer Stéphan Lorti
Recorded by Paul Campagne and Davy Gallant at Studio King and Dogger Pond Studio
Mixed and Mastered by Davy Gallant at Dogger Pond Studio

Coral Egan appears courtesy of Justin Time Records
Patrick Watson appears courtesy of Secret City Records
Thomas Hellman appears courtesy of Spectra Musique

Thank you to Véronique Croisile, Olivier Sirois, Justin West, Florence Bélanger, Bruno Robitaille,
Francyne Furtado, David Murphy, Mona Cochingyan and Connie Kaldor

ISBN-10: 2-923163-56-7 / ISBN-13: 978-2-923163-56-7

Ⓟ 2009 Folle Avoine Productions

Ⓒ 2009 Les Éditions Le vent qui vire, Lac Laplume Music